D0607340

Derting, Kimberly,
Vivi loves science /
[2021]
33305249782172
ca   08/18/21

ERTING and SHELLI R. JOHANNES

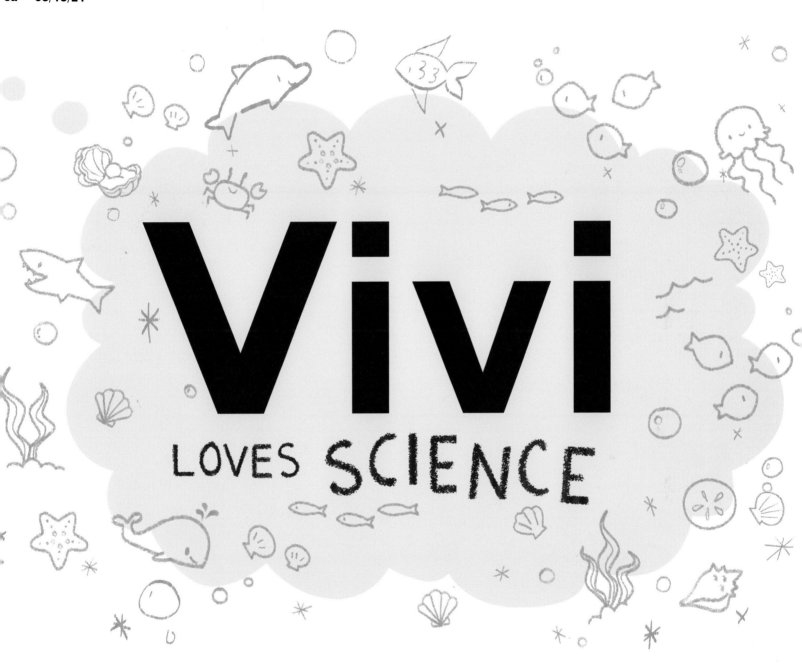

Vivi
LOVES SCIENCE

Illustrations by
JOELLE MURRAY

Greenwillow Books. *An Imprint of* HarperCollins*Publishers*

Vivi loved science. She loved learning about nature and planet Earth. She especially loved the ocean and everything that lives in it.

That's why Vivi was excited.

Today her science class was going to the beach.

Vivi sat next to her lab partner, Graeme, on the bus. She made a list of things she wanted to investigate when they got there.

"I hope we see a dolphin," she said. "Did you know that some dolphins can stay underwater for up to fifteen minutes?"

"Wow," said Graeme. "I wish I could do that."

When they arrived at the shore, their science teacher, Ms. Cousteau, said, "Today we're to going study tide pools. We might spot starfish, crabs, or even a jellyfish."

Vivi raised her hand. "Did you know that jellyfish have lived on Earth longer than dinosaurs and sharks?"

"That's true," said Ms. Cousteau. "Jellyfish have been around for at least 500 million years! Scientists think they are the oldest animals on our planet."

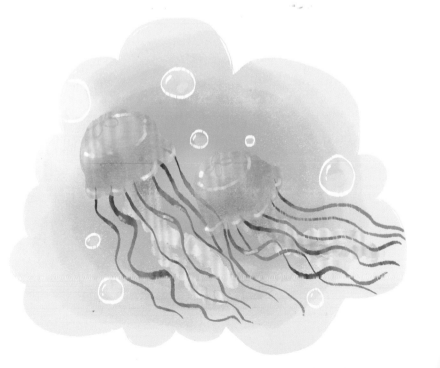

"Sharks have only been here for about 400 million years," said Vivi.

"Are sharks fish?" asked Graeme.

"Yes," Ms. Cousteau said. "Sharks are fish because they breathe underwater."

40 feet!

6 inches!

"Did you know that the biggest shark is called a whale shark?" said Vivi. "Whale sharks can be forty feet long!"

"What's the smallest shark?" asked Mia.

"The dwarf lantern shark," said Vivi. "They are six inches long, and their bellies light up!"

"Right!" said Ms. Cousteau. "You'll be a great marine biologist someday, Vivi."

"Now, let's make aquascopes so we all can see underwater," said Ms. Cousteau.
Everyone raced over to picnic tables, where a park ranger was setting out supplies.

Graeme decorated his aquascope with duct tape.

Vivi glued some seashells around the edge of hers.

"This looks fin-tastic!" she said.

Make Your Own Aquascope

MATERIALS:

* One large waterproof container (a plastic yogurt or oatmeal container, a half-gallon milk carton, or a coffee can) with both ends removed

* Clear plastic wrap

* Rubber bands or heavy-duty tape

* Scissors

* String (optional)

* Black paint (optional)

* Shells, sand, and other decorations (optional)

STEPS:

* Cut off both ends of your container with your scissors. This should only be done with help from an adult!

* Stretch plastic wrap over one end of your container and secure it in place with sturdy rubber bands or heavy-duty tape.

* Trim the excess plastic.

Ranger Earle led them through the dunes to the beach.
Vivi and her friends were careful to stay on the path,
away from the nesting birds and delicate grasses.

"Does anyone know how a tide pool is created?" Ranger
Earle asked.

Vivi raised her hand. "When the tide comes in, water
collects in pools that plants and animals can live in.
When the tide goes out, the pools are still there."

"You got it!" said Ranger Earle. "The tide is low now,
so we should have lots of tide pools to investigate."

"Everyone work with your lab partner," said
Ms. Cousteau. "And be sure to record what
you find on your scavenger hunt worksheet."

"Let's look for a big pool," said Vivi to Graeme.
They raced toward the rocks.

"There's one!" Graeme pointed to a large pool of water. "You go first, and I'll record the data."

Vivi peered into the water with her aquascope. "Wow!" she said. "I think I see an anemone!"

Graeme checked off "sea anemone" on the list.

BEACH SCAVENGER HUNT CHECKLIST

Partners: Vivi & Graeme

Work together with your lab partner to find the following things:

Barnacles
Clams
Crab
Eel

Jellyfish
Mussels
✓ Sea Anemone
Sea Urchin

Seashells
Seaweed
Snails
Starfish

Vivi called out each animal she spotted.

"Snails!"

"Baby clams!"

"Barnacles!"

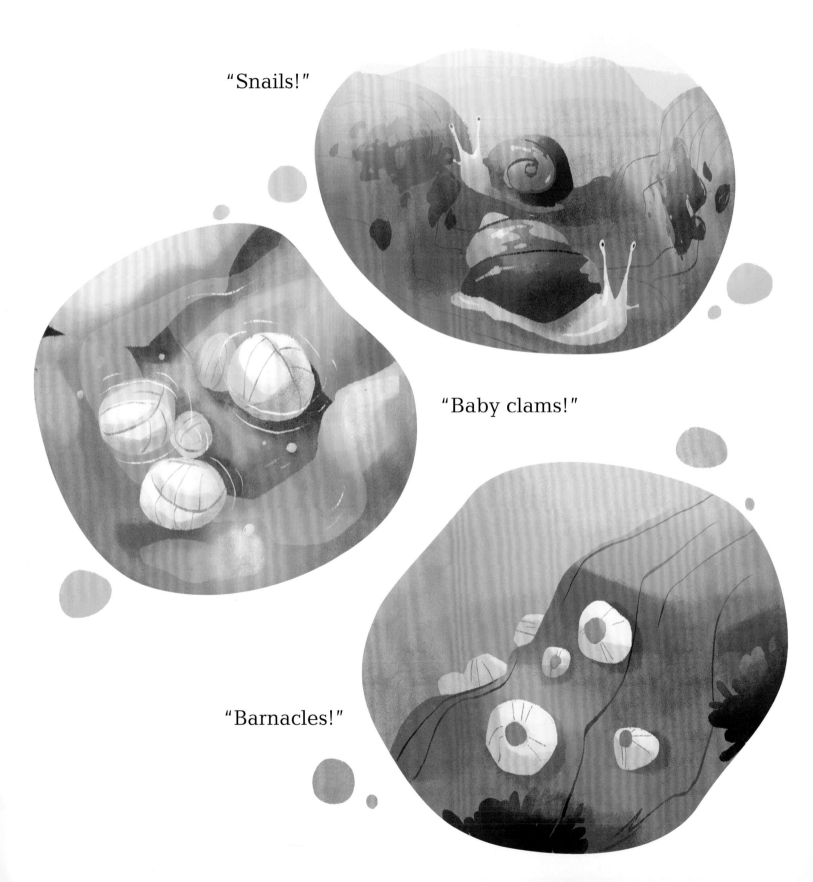

"Four hermit crabs!"

"A minnow!"

"Do you see any plants?"
Graeme asked.

"There's some seaweed
and algae," Vivi said.

"Do you want to look?"

Graeme put his aquascope into the water. "Mussels!
A starfish! A sea urchin! There are tons of shells, too!"

Vivi spotted a big seashell near the tide pool. She picked it up and held it to her ear. "This sounds just like the ocean," she said. "But it's really air traveling through the shell."

Graeme listened, too. "Sounds like waves to me," he said.

"I wonder who lived in this shell," said Vivi.

"Maybe a giant crab," said Graeme.

"Let's put it back," said Vivi. "So someone will move in again."

Vivi pointed at a flat rock, closer to the water's edge.
"Let's see if anything lives under there!" she said.
"It's an excellent hiding place," said Graeme. "Maybe
we'll even spot an eel."
Together, Vivi and Graeme turned over the rock.

"What's that?" said Graeme. "It looks like a toad."

"Look! Over here! We found a huge fish!" Vivi yelled.

The entire class raced over to see what Vivi and Graeme had discovered in the tide pool.

"We need to get that fish back into the ocean," said Mia. "It's running out of water."

"Wait, I don't think we should touch it," Vivi said.
"You're right, Vivi," Ms. Cousteau said. "Let's ask
the ranger. She'll know what to do."

"That is a plainfin midshipman," Ranger Earle said. "This fish buries itself in wet sand and mud when protecting its nest."

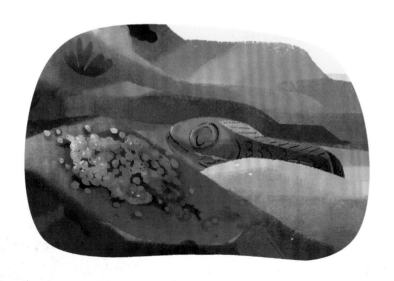

Graeme pointed to the little orange circles stuck to the bottom of the rock. "What's that stuff?" "Those must be her eggs," said Vivi. "Actually, those are *his* eggs," Ranger Earle explained.

"His?" Mia asked.
"Yes, the dad stays with
the nest until the eggs
hatch," Ranger Earle said.

"How long does that take?" Vivi asked.
"The dad protects and cleans the eggs for
weeks and weeks," said Ranger Earle.
"Sometimes there are hundreds of eggs!"
"I'm glad we didn't move him," said Mia.

"You were right not to move him," said Ranger Earle.
"Whenever we're in nature, it's important to look at
animals and not touch."
"Plus, this is his home, and we're just visitors," Vivi said.

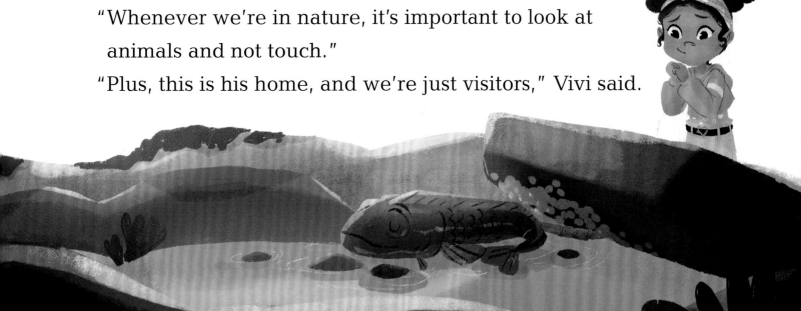

Ranger Earle led the class along the water's edge.
They spotted something lying on the sand.
"What is that?" asked Mia.
"Be careful! That's a jellyfish," Ranger Earle said.

"Do they bite?" Graeme asked.

"No, jellyfish don't have teeth," Vivi said.

"Right! Most jellyfish have tentacles like this one,"
   Ranger Earle said. "They can still sting when they're
   out of the water."

"Before you leave, you can each pick one shell to take home,"
Ranger Earle said. "Just make sure it's empty."
Vivi and Graeme hunted for the perfect shells.

Graeme found
a white scallop
shell.

But Vivi kept searching until she found something unexpected. "A shark tooth!" she said.

"Good eyes!" Ranger Earle said, inspecting Vivi's treasure.
"Is that tooth 400 million years old?" asked Graeme.
"Probably not," said Ranger Earle. "But it could be a hundred years old."

As the class headed back to the bus, Vivi and Graeme
took one last look at the ocean.

"I think I see a shark!" Graeme shouted.

Just then, something big jumped out of the water.

"It's a dolphin," said Vivi. "No, it's a whole dolphin family!"

Vivi smiled. She loved field trips and the ocean, and she
loved science best of all!

Vivi's Science Facts

- **Aquascope**—An underwater viewing device. You can build your own!

- **Beach**—The part of the shore covered with sand or pebbles at an ocean or a lake. I love the beach!

- **Ms. Cousteau**—My science teacher. She has the same last name as a super-famous French undersea explorer named Jacques Cousteau.

- **Dolphin**—Dolphins look like huge fish, but they are actually mammals. They breathe air and are super smart. Dolphins are my favorite animals!

- **Dunes**—Ridges of sand created by the wind and/or water. Dunes can be found in deserts or near lakes and oceans.

- **Sylvia Earle**—A famous marine biologist who has led more than one hundred expeditions and spent more than 7,000 hours under the sea.

- **Jellyfish**—Did you know that jellyfish aren't made of jelly and aren't even fish? They are marine invertebrates, which means they don't have spines. Jellyfish are one of the oldest animals on Earth!

- **Marine biologist**—Someone who studies all life in the ocean. I want to be a marine biologist!

- **Nest**—A shelter made by an animal for its eggs and young. Most people think nests are only for birds, but we found the plainfin midshipman in his nest.

- **Ocean**—A ginormous body of salt water. There are five oceans on our planet: Pacific, Atlantic, Indian, Southern, and Arctic.

- **Plainfin midshipman**—Sometimes called the "toad fish." The dad fish is in charge of guarding the eggs until they hatch.

- **Science**—A system of observations and experiments used to ask and answer questions about the natural world. I love science!

- **Seashell**—A hard, protective case created by an animal that lives in the ocean.

- **Shark**—A fast-swimming fish that lives in salt water. Like jellyfish, sharks don't have bones . . . but they DO have lots of teeth!

- **Tide**—In most places, there are two high tides and two low tides a day. *High tide* is when the water is highest. *Low tide* is when the water level is lowest—this is the best time to find tide pools. Did you know that tides are caused by the moon, the sun, and gravity? Cool, right?

- **Tide pool**—When the tide comes in, water collects in small pools of different sizes and depths. Plants and animals live in these pools, surviving as the tide goes in and out.

- **Waves**—Most ocean waves are caused by wind. Sometimes, waves start thousands of miles offshore.

To LR & LP for always encouraging us to follow our dreams—K. D. & S. R. J.

For mom and dad—my love for you both is deeper than all of the oceans combined!—J. M.

Vivi says, "Experimenting with science is fun, but remember that safety comes first, and always make sure a grown-up is there to help if you need it!"

Vivi Loves Science. Text copyright © 2021 by Kimberly Derting and Shelli R. Johannes.Illustrations copyright © 2021 by Joelle Murray. All rights reserved. Manufactured in Italy. For information address HarperCollins Children's Books, a division of HarperCollins Publishers, 195 Broadway, New York, NY 10007. www.harpercollinschildrens.com.
The full-color art was created in Adobe Photoshop™. The text type is Candida.

Library of Congress Cataloging-in-Publication Data
Names: Derting, Kimberly, author. | Johannes, Shelli R., author. | Murray, Joelle, illustrator. Title: Vivi loves science / written by Kimberly Derting and Shelli R. Johannes ; illustrated by Joelle Murray. Description: First edition. | New York, NY : Greenwillow Books, an Imprint of HarperCollins Publishers, [2021] | Audience: Ages 4–8. | Audience: Grades K–1. | Summary: "Vivi and her classmates take a field trip to the beach to study tide pools" — Provided by publisher. Includes a scavenger hunt checklist, science facts, and instructions for making an aquascope.
Identifiers: LCCN 2020051382 | ISBN 9780062946065 (hardcover)
Subjects: CYAC: Tide pools—Fiction. | School field trips—Fiction.
Classification: LCC PZ7.D4468 Viv 2021 | DDC [E]—dc23 LC record available at https://lccn.loc.gov/2020051382
21 22 23 24 25 RTLO 10 9 8 7 6 5 4 3 2 1 First Edition   Greenwillow Books

Make Your Own Tide Pool

(A fun experiment to try no matter where you live! Remember to always return any living animals to their habitats when you are done.)

MATERIALS:

* Dishpan, plastic bin, bucket, or other large container

* Seashells and rocks (check your local craft store for decorative shells, sand dollars, and starfish if you don't live near the beach)

* Sand or pebbles

* Toy sea creatures such as turtles, starfish, crabs, octopus, snails, etc. (you can make your own, or buy plastic mini animals at stores)

* Pitcher or cups

DIRECTIONS:

1. Fill your container with rocks and sand.

2. Arrange the rocks to create a pool.

3. Place your animals and plants into the pool.

4. Slowly add water.

5. Continue adding water until you reach "high tide."

6. After observing, remove water one cup at a time.

7. Continue removing water until you've reached "low tide."

DISCUSSION QUESTIONS:

1. Low tide: Which animals will be exposed to the air first? Why?

2. High tide: Which animals will be exposed to water first? Why?

3. When are most animals exposed to air?

4. When are most animals exposed to water?

5. What features do animals use to help them during the tide changes?

Surf's up!